Rosey ...

the imperfect angel

the first in a series about the beauties which lie hidden beneath the defects

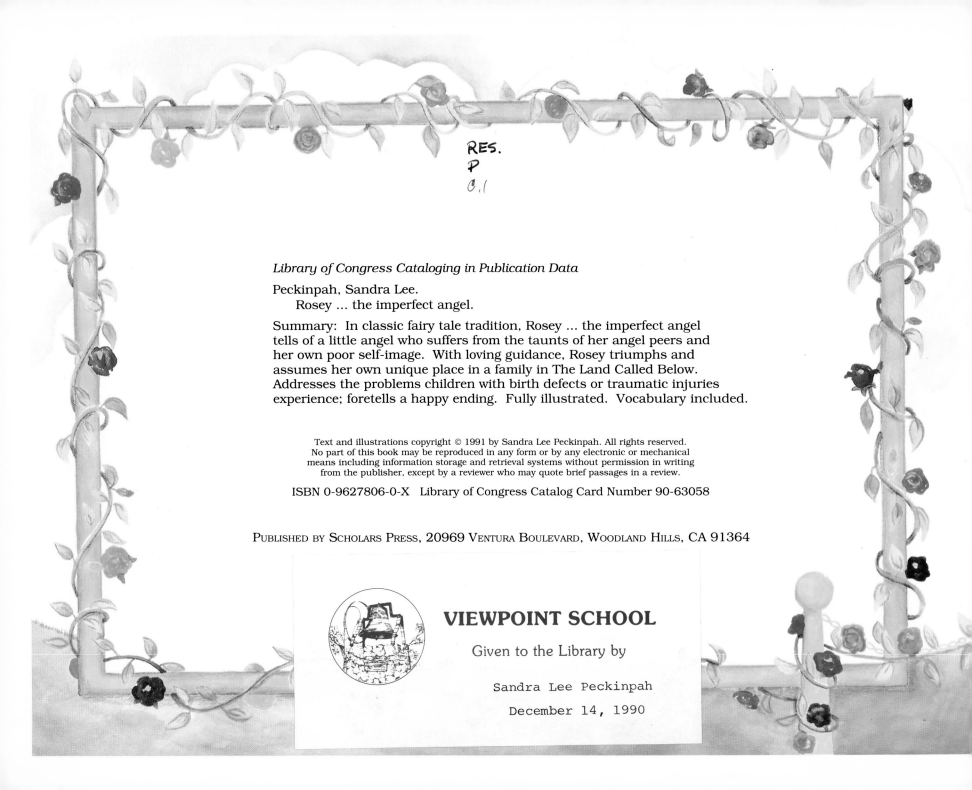

Library of Congress Cataloging in Publication Data

Peckinpah, Sandra Lee.
  Rosey ... the imperfect angel.

Summary: In classic fairy tale tradition, Rosey ... the imperfect angel tells of a little angel who suffers from the taunts of her angel peers and her own poor self-image. With loving guidance, Rosey triumphs and assumes her own unique place in a family in The Land Called Below. Addresses the problems children with birth defects or traumatic injuries experience; foretells a happy ending. Fully illustrated. Vocabulary included.

ISBN 0-9627806-0-X   Library of Congress Catalog Card Number 90-63058

PUBLISHED BY SCHOLARS PRESS, 20969 VENTURA BOULEVARD, WOODLAND HILLS, CA 91364

Rosey ... *the imperfect angel*

by Sandra Lee Peckinpah

Illustrated by Trisha Moore

Every year all over this world boys and girls are born with birth defects. Every year all over this world children suffer accident or disease which robs them of some integral physical asset or ability to see, hear, speak, or walk. Beneath all of these traumas, whatever their form or shape, lie the beautiful hearts and noble souls of these boys and girls. It is these hidden beauties which the world must see. **Rosey ... the imperfect angel** is dedicated to these special, beautiful children and their families.

Sandra Lee Peckinpah
Westlake Village, California 1991

"Something's up!" said the little boy with skyward eyes.

"It certainly feels very different ... nothing like it was before," said the puzzled mother as she clasped both hands under her very round tummy. She, too, gazed up at The Blue.

The Land Called Above demanded attention as playful, cumulus clouds soared and vibrant lights slashed through the cloud holes.

"I feel it, too!" said the astonished father, taking a deep breath of the electric air as he affectionately patted his wife's very round tummy.

"I can hardly wait to find out what it is!" said the older brother, clapping his hands with excitement and expectation.

At the very moment the family
in The Land Called Below
noticed the changes in the sky,
a dozen little angels scurried about
in The Land Called Above.
"Something's up!"
"Something's up!"
"Something's definitely up!"
the little angels shouted
to each other.
April Showers
flicked several raindrops
at each of them.
"Sh ... sh ... sh ...," she admonished.
"Boss Angel is on his way!"

Boss Angel! The little angels dashed to their work.
Chilly February furiously planted a wheelbarrow of fresh pansies and
strawberries. "I wish I had that Groundhog Gauge from The Land Called Below!" she muttered. Breezy March
whisked away weeds and dead leaves. May Flowers scurried to her fragrant boughs; June Beetles tidied up her
vegetable beds and flicked away the pixieflies; Snapdragon skipped among her July blooms; Marigold August
smiled with satisfaction at her perfect flower beds; stately September Maple Leaf surveyed her brilliant trees.

"Give me a hand with this thing!"
Pumpkin Pie screeched,
"It weighs a ton!"
She labored to roll
the huge orange
squash through
October's gates.
Nuttilia Brown
November,
known as "Nuttie,"
gathered baskets of
walnuts and acorns;
Frosty December laced
another pine tree with snow.

As the fog
cleared in Central Park,
Boss Angel surveyed the entrances
to the twelve gardens. Tiny buds hung
from golden vines that climbed over each arbor.
Obediently, each little angel respectfully made way for Boss Angel.
March discreetly kicked a stray leaf under a stepping stone.
At the far end of the circle all that could be seen were
masses of bloomless twigs and gnarled leafless branches
covered with sharp black thorns. Boss Angel frowned.
"And where is Rosey?" he demanded.
Eleven little angels lowered their eyes to their tiny feet.

Far off on a distant rain cloud one little angel pulled her gossamer wings tightly about her. One of the eleven other little angels thought she heard the sound of weeping.

"Why, Rosey!" called Boss Angel.
"Is that you crying?
Whatever is the matter,
my little rosebud?"

"Boss Angel!" Rosey said in a startled voice with her head bowed.
"Sometimes … sometimes …
I … I … I just feel so different."

Boss Angel walked toward her,
lifted her down
from her little cloud,
and placed his hand
under her chin.
He tilted her little face
upwards and spoke to her
kindly and affectionately.
If the truth were known,
Rosey had always been his favorite.
"Rosey, my dear, you *are* different,
perfectly different,"
Boss Angel told her softly.
"Now, don't you worry.
Sometimes even here
in our lovely gardens,
the greatest challenges
bring the greatest rewards.
Rosey, my dear, all will
soon be revealed to you."

Rosey's face remained tilted toward the sunlight which shone down through the clouds and dried the tears on her lovely little face. Her countenance was different, for her upper lip was divided, and on one side it curled up toward her little pink nose, looking for all the world just like a rose petal! Of course, this was the real reason Boss Angel had christened her Rosey the very first time he had seen her. Rosey would never forget that moment.

The other angels had gathered around her to see her funny mouth. They had all tittered gleefully every time she took a deep breath of air, for she had whistled and snorted helplessly. Oh! How the other angels had laughed and laughed. Rosey had tried hard not to show that they had hurt her feelings. Boss Angel had hurried over as soon as he heard the mimicking, snickering sounds the other angels had made.

"Snort! Snort!" and "Oink! Oink!" eleven little angels had screeched. September's Maple Leaf had drawn herself up haughtily. "She sounds just like a little piglet!" The other little angels had doubled over in fits of laughter. Rosey had said not a word. She had been far too busy desperately trying to hold her breath.

"Stop!" Boss Angel had yelled. Rosey had been so startled by the anger in his voice that suddenly the air she had been frantically trying to control had exploded from her rosebud lips. Out had come the sound of a giant "S ... N ... O ... R ... R ... R ... T !" Two of the angels had covered their perfect little mouths with their tiny hands to squelch their giggles. "NOT ANOTHER SOUND!" Boss Angel had admonished them. Every single angel had become very, very still. They were not at all used to Boss Angel's raising his voice.

Boss Angel had walked slowly around Rosey. A blossoming smile had appeared on his dignified face. "Oh, good," Snapdragon had whispered. "He's not mad any more." The sound of gossamer wings had filled the air as all the angels gathered around Boss Angel. "My little angels, today is a day of celebration. I must name our newest angel just as I named each of you when you came here to our gardens." The little angels had nodded. "Yes! Yes! We remember."

Boss Angel had placed his hand under the chin of the littlest angel and tilted her face upwards. "Your mouth is as lovely as a rose petal sparkling with dew. I hereby declare your name to be Rosey. You shall be First Angel and your domain is to be the Garden of January."

The other angels had gasped! Such an honor for the smallest and the newest and the most different of them all! Breezy March had muttered, "First Angel! She'll find out soon enough that she has the hardest job of all. Why, everyone knows how rare it is to see the green of a leaf or the bud of a flower in January." March whipped some windblown wisps of hair away from her face. "Finally, somebody has a job that's harder than mine."

A flash of lightning ended Rosey's daydreaming. She smiled her crooked smile as she remembered how thankful she had been to Boss Angel. That was the last time any of the angels had ever teased her about the shape of her mouth.

But there was work to be done, and little Rosey put away her memories and flew out of her rain cloud toward her garden. She parted the golden vines at January's entrance, and as she looked at the masses of brown twigs with their sharp, black thorns, and the piles and piles of dead leaves, she sighed. "Boss Angel was right. I do have quite a challenge."

But Rosey remembered what Boss Angel had told her, that all would soon be revealed, and she set about diligently tending her garden. Rainbows arched through the skies, full moons waxed and waned. The smiling sun hurried the frost away to his winter kingdom, but still Rosey's January garden, although ever so much neater, remained filled with the same brown twigs, black thorns, and piles and piles of dead leaves.

One bright day Rosey felt the
wind against her cheek.
She danced from garden to garden
to see what the other angels were doing.
She liked to admire their flowers and trees
and she always had an encouraging word
for each little angel gardener.
The sight of their abundant blooms
and the sweet fragrance
of their flowers warmed
her happy little heart.
But today something
was different.
"There's magic in the air!
Something's up!
Something's up!"
she sang.

She didn't have to wait long.
With the crackle of lightning
and the rolling of thunder, Boss Angel
swept into Central Park.
He loved making a grand entrance!
"Gather close, my little angels.
We have an important mission to fill
in The Land Called Below."
His voice was kind but
his tone was very firm.
"At the next lunar celebration,
I want you to bring me bouquets and baskets
of the most glorious gatherings from your gardens.
The angel who has worked the hardest
and achieved the most glorious results
will be the angel whom I shall choose
to fulfill an important mission in
The Land Called Below."
And with that,
Boss Angel vanished.

A confident May Flowers smiled to herself. "I'm certain to be chosen," she cooed. April Showers, overhearing May's comment, scrambled up her tiny ladder and looked over at May's garden. "That all depends on me, doesn't it? After all, everyone knows that 'April Showers bring May flowers!'" Chilly February paid no attention. Her pansies were blooming and her strawberry plants were well established. Marigold August considered planting another row of azure cockle bells to add to her yellow blooms. Snapdragon wasn't worried. She already had all the colors of the rainbow among the massed blooms of her garden that stood tall and open to the sun.

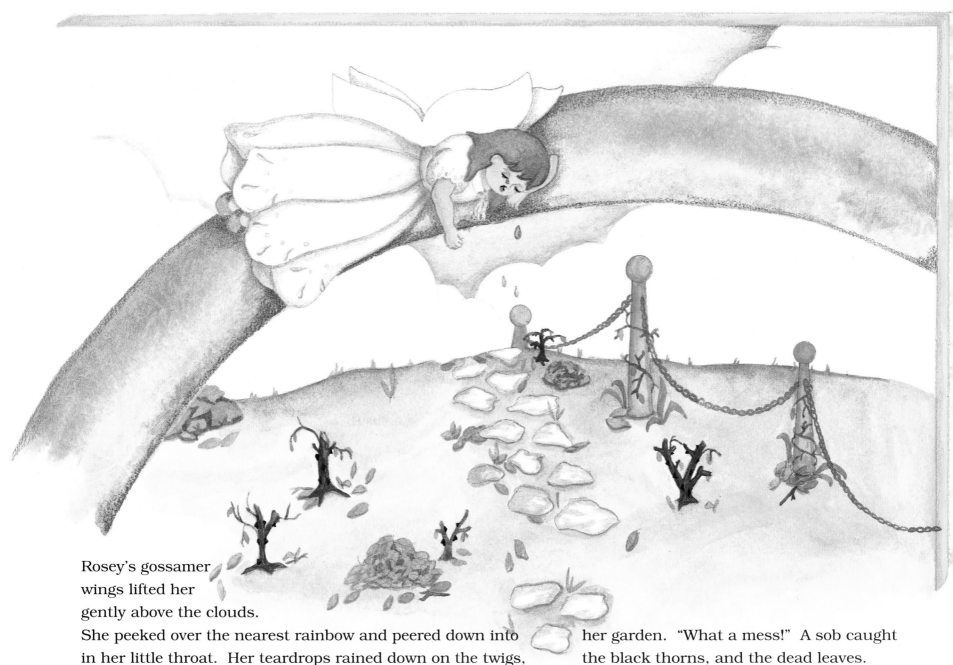

Rosey's gossamer
wings lifted her
gently above the clouds.
She peeked over the nearest rainbow and peered down into her garden. "What a mess!" A sob caught in her little throat. Her teardrops rained down on the twigs, the black thorns, and the dead leaves.
A despondent little Rosey alighted next to one of her frostbitten rose bushes and wept into the tangled mass.
She felt sorry for herself. "Whatever am I to do? I … I … I have a garden that won't bl … bl … bloom … and a face that is different from any of my sisters. I'll never be the chosen one."

When Rosey opened her swollen eyes,
she noticed that her tear drops had covered
each bush with a gentle rain shower.
She opened her eyes wide.
"Could something be up?"
The twigs did look different.
"Could that be the green of a leaf?"
she thought in amazement
as something green
and truly fresh
popped discreetly
from the bend in the twig.

"Is that the bud of a rose?" she said aloud as she saw a hint of crimson emerging between two black thorns. It was true! Where each tear had landed, the bushes she had loved and protected had responded in the only way they could. The tiny green leaves and the infant buds manifested the love that the littlest angel had truly bestowed on all those twigs and black thorns.

"My garden is blooming! My garden is blooming!"
Rosey danced around each twig and watched it
turn green. She was so elated that she hugged
the bush thorns and all, and planted a kiss
upon the tiny rosebud. Suddenly, each
petal began to curl back, gently
exposing the next petal, and the next,
until the flower was in full bloom!
Every bush joined in and Rosey
danced about her garden, welcoming
and praising each and every rose.
These were no ordinary roses.
They had a special look of their own.
Some had a curled petal or two.
Some bloomed in colors that
Rosey had never seen before.
She could not believe her eyes!

Boss Angel was, of course, delighted to declare Rosey The Chosen One, for indeed her roses had produced the most glorious blooms in any of the gardens. Even her sister angels commended her for her remarkable triumph. They could clearly see that Rosey's blooms, imperfect though they were, had captured the uniqueness of the sunbeams and the glory of the stars. Like Rosey, their differences defined their beauty. "You see, my little Rosey," Boss Angel told her, "you have met a great challenge. You had the ability within you all along." His face glowed with pride.

"Your reward is an even greater challenge.
I have every confidence in you, my little rosebud.
You must now go to a special garden in
The Land Called Below. There you will
have a joyful life as you bring this
special family's garden to full bloom.
You, little Rosey, more than anyone,
can teach them the beauty of
imperfection." Boss Angel tilted
her face toward the sunlight and
kissed her tiny little nose.
Rosey thought she
detected a tear in his eye.
Boss Angel raised his arm
and beckoned to the heavens.
A shining cloud answered
his call and wrapped itself
gently around Rosey as
Boss Angel and the eleven
little angels waved good-bye.

"Good-bye, Rosey ... we love you,"
they called, their voices echoing
through the clouds in a song.

At that very moment the little boy in The Land Called Below shouted, "It's shining up! It's that special feeling again. Something's up! It's shining up!"

The family in The Land Called Below
gathered around their new baby.
The mother's loving arms held
her new infant, and the father's
loving eyes smiled down at the baby
with the crooked little rosebud mouth,
and the brothers exclaimed,
"She's the most beautiful
little girl in all the land!"

With special love and thanks...

... to Wendy Steinmetz, for planting the seed of an idea

... to Robert H. Barnhard, M. D., who steered me to the right garden

... to Ellen "Binky" Petok, C.L.C., for helping me nurture "my little Rosey"

... to Janet Salomonson, M.D., Leslie Holve, M.D., and the Saint John's Hospital Cleft Palate team
   in Santa Monica, California, for bringing my daughter's face to full bloom

... to David, Garrett, and Trevor, for the unconditional love that allowed me the magic of tears

... to all those little baby angel gardeners who gave me a new look at perfection -
   Tonya, Preston, Michael, Spencer, and others whose names I do not know

... and most of all, to my daughter, Julianne Belle, for choosing me as her special mother
   and teaching me the beauty and the joy of imperfection

Sandra Lee Peckinpah

A HANDY, EASY TO USE VOCABULARY GUIDE FOR

Rosey ... the imperfect angel

All young children love to learn new words! One of the great joys and benefits of reading is to build a strong vocabulary. The author is pleased to include this glossary for all of *Rosey's* readers who enjoy learning new words as they turn the pages of a favorite story.

abundant	adj.	very plentiful, more than enough
admonished	v.	scolded, chastised
alighted	v.	settled on
arbor	n.	an arch covered with vines or branches
asset	n.	something of value
astonished	adj.	very surprised
azure	adj.	a beautiful blue!
beckoned	v.	called
bestowed	v.	gave
boughs	n.	branches of a tree or bush
challenge	n.	a demand that you do your very best
christened	v.	gave a name to
cleft palate	ph.	a narrow divison in the roof of the mouth and/or lip when two parts of the palate fail to join properly
cockle bells	adj., n.	a beautiful plant with blue flowers
commended	v.	praised
cooed	v.	spoken in a soft murmur
countenance	n.	the full expression on a person's face
crimson	n.	deep red
cumulus	n.	clouds made up of rounded heaps from a flat base
declare	v.	say, speak positively
defect	n.	a blemish or an imperfection
defined	v.	made the meaning very clear
desperately	adv.	hopelessly
despondent	adj.	discouraged, dejected, sad
detected	v.	saw
dignified	adj.	noble, stately
diligently	adv.	very hard working
discreetly	adv.	carefully, sensibly
domain	n.	land under the control of one person
elated	adj.	joyful

emerging	v.	showing, coming out
established	v.	set up permanently
exclaimed	v.	spoke firmly with strong feeling
expectation	n.	hope
exposing	v.	showing
fragrance *(fragrant)*	n. *(adj.)*	pleasant odor, nice smell
frantically	adv.	excitedly, wildly
frostbitten	adj.	injured by severe cold
gauge	n.	an instrument which measures
gleefully	adv.	joyously, merrily
gnarled	adj.	knotted, twisted
gossamer	adj.	very light and thin, like a cobweb
haughtily	adv.	overly proud, scornfully
imperfect	adj.	not perfect (but nonetheless beautiful!)
integral	adj.	needed, necessary
laced	v.	to trim or beautify, adorn
lunar	adj.	of the moon
manifested	v.	showed plainly or clearly
mimicking	n.	the act of imitating
mission	n.	very special job
muttered	v.	complained, grumbled
noble	adj.	of very fine character, good
peered	v.	looked closely
pixieflies	n.	tiny little insects
praising	v.	saying words of approval
remarkable	adj.	very special
responded	v.	answered
revealed	v.	shown to you, made plain
scurried	v.	walked or ran quickly
skyward	adj./adv.	towards the sky
snickering	n.	half hidden disrespectful laughing
squelch	v.	stop, cause to end
stately	adj.	dignified, grand
surveyed	v.	looked about very carefully
tending	v.	taking special care of
tidied	v.	made neat and orderly
tilted	v.	slanted or leaned upward
tittered	v.	laughed lightly
trauma	n.	a wound or injury and its effect
triumph	n.	victory
uniqueness	n.	something very, very special, unusual
vibrant	adj.	very colorful
waxed and waned	v.	came and went, arrived and left
whisked	v.	swept or brushed quickly
wisps	n.	small locks of hair